ONE LITTLE TREE

ONE LITTLE TREE

A Christmas Card
of a Finnish Landscape

by

E. M. ALMEDINGEN

illustrated by

DENISE BROWN

W · W · NORTON & COMPANY · INC
NEW YORK

To Lucy Lunt
in love and friendship

CONTENTS

CHAPTER I

Arni plans a birthday surprise

Yes, this story is all about a Christmas tree, but it really began in June, and the summer can be very hot in Finland. On that day the heat lay like a blanket over grass, tree and shrub. Arni, a thin grey linen smock over him, lay sprawling on the floor of the tiny summer house at the bottom of a small garden. Sunlight rippled over a mound of copper coins on a low bench. Arni had already counted them twice over, but he meant to count them again. He must be really sure he had enough for Kesti's birthday present.

He knew he had no business to be in the summer house at all.

He was supposed to be on the uplands beyond the fir wood outside his home, gathering bilberries for his mother to make jam, and two empty baskets stood by the door. Arni had decided that the bilberries could wait until it got a bit cooler.

But Biki, a huge, grey and tan mongrel of very mixed origins, started thumping his tail impatiently.

'Wait a minute,' said Arni, 'I must count the money again. One, three and four, that makes eight, and another four makes twelve. Here are five more. Does it make twenty? It did last time, but I am afraid I am wrong –' Arni shook his tousled flaxen head and started all over again.

He knew perfectly well that he could run back to the house and ask his mother, and she would know how much he had. But Arni would not do it. In the first place, he knew she expected him back with the bilberries. Secondly and much more importantly, Arni clung to his 'secret'. Nobody was to know that he had been saving for months to get Kesti a birthday present. Arni lived for his 'secrets'. They were at once an adventure and a game, something even more exciting than a fight at school. Once he started carrying a 'secret' in his mind, Arni felt as though he had got to the very top of a tall tree and could take delight in a wider landscape than his daily life afforded him.

So nobody must know what he had planned for Kesti's birthday. He knew that she wanted a box of coloured glass beads, and he meant to buy them, though Arni felt rather scornful about the beads. Kesti, five years old to his eight, was too small to use a needle and thread. Their mother would have to turn those beads into necklaces and bracelets which – in Arni's eyes – were stupid

8

and useless things which could please nobody but little girls who did not know any better. But Kesti had seen someone sporting such a bracelet, and had been talking about it ever since. Arni had promised nothing, but he was determined she should have her beads.

He had the money. He also had a plan of campaign. They lived about two miles away from Raino, the nearest village, and Raino had a shop which sold little except candles, salt, sugar, stamps, hemp and cattle medicines. Therefore, within the next fortnight he must somehow or other get his father to take him to Bielostrov, the nearest town to their home. It had a railway station, two or three churches, and one paved street full of most fascinating shops, as Arni thought. On rare occasions the timber-merchant, for whom his father worked, sent him there on business, and three times Arni had been allowed to go. The railway station fascinated him, but the shops mattered most. His own pockets empty, Arni spent his time window-gazing. Even a glass of hot, spiced milk and a bun at the baker's did not excite Arni as much as that make-believe shopping. There he stood, gazing and choosing in a grand manner – as though his pockets were full of money – a scarf for his mother, a doll for Kesti, a new collar for Biki, a pocket-knife for himself.

But it was now summer, and all those excursions to Bielostrov took place in the winter when the frost of Finnish December bit so deep that even sheepskins, snowboots and thick gauntlets did not seem warm enough. His father's business finished, they would leave the paved street for the open country outside and march towards the Baroness's Wood for what Arni considered to be the

9

most important business of the year. There, his father would choose and cut down a Christmas tree. This was done with the Baroness's permission. No *yelkas* of the right size and shape grew anywhere in the immediate neighbourhood of Arni's home. His father always said:

'Bless the Baroness for her kind heart! Where would our Christmas be without a tree, and where else could we find it?'

Arni had never met the Baroness. He had no idea where she lived, but he felt that he knew her well because of that annual excursion to the wood she owned, and he knew too that a Christmas without a tree would hardly be like a real Christmas. A large gilt star fixed to the very tip of the top frond meant the coming of the Child. What would Christmas be unless the Child came into the house? Arni could not even imagine it.

Having cut the little tree, his father would carry it carefully back to Bielostrov, to the corner of the market place where he had left the pony and the sledge, and they would drive home across a still, snow-mantled world, every tree so beautiful that you caught your breath as you looked at it.

Arni knew that they would go to Bielostrov in the winter to cut down their tree. But now it was June, and how could he expect his father to take him at such a busy time of the year when all the hands at the timber-yard were kept at work from dawn till long after sunset.

'I do wish Kesti had been born at Christmas,' he thought. 'One of the boys at school was ill and they took him to see a doctor at Bielostrov, but I am quite well, and it would not help if I were to cut my hand or bruise a knee – Mother would see to it. I wonder what people do to get really ill. But then I couldn't do any shopping if I got sick. No, there's nothing for it – I shall have to tell Father why I want to go. It'll still be a secret for Kesti – I know he won't tell.'

Here Biki lost his patience and pushed his huge shaggy head against Arni's knee.

'What a fidget you are,' Arni grumbled and, scooping up the coins, he put them into a little wooden box. In a moment, he was running through the thick spinney of spruce and fir, towards the uplands, to get the bilberries for the jam, and the whole wood echoed with Biki's happy barking.

CHAPTER 2

The end of Arni's secret

Because of the heat, Anna, Arni's mother, thought they had better eat out of doors that Sunday, and her husband carried the square deal table into the yard which lay at right angles to the trim grey-timbered little house. The yard had no fencing. In one corner three old limes and an enormous fir offered shade, and just behind the trees a brook threaded its silver singing way into the river running past the wood to the south of the steading.

Arni's eyes lit up when his mother carried out a big tureen full of cold cucumber soup. It was his favourite food, but they did not have it often because, as Anna said, it took so long to prepare and she was always busy. But today there it was, thick and creamy-green, and the tureen was full to the brim. Arni hoped that he might have two bowls of it. He sat down happily and did not pull Kesti's plaits when she threw wilted mullein petals into his face.

The bowl emptied, Arni was just going to ask for more when he realized that his parents, their own food barely touched, were deep in talk. Nils's face was drawn and Anna's blue eyes were full of bewilderment. Arni put down his empty bowl and listened.

'Are you quite sure that Raino will be all right?' Anna was asking. 'The Russians won't come here and take everything away, will they?'

'Oh no, Raino is all right – the boundary has been settled,' Nils replied, 'but I can't help being worried. All the timber at Bielostrov and elsewhere is as good as gone now, and there will be no more business for us down south.'

Anna picked up her spoon and tried to eat. But Arni saw that her hand was shaking.

'It is wicked the way these wars and revolutions upset everything to nobody's good,' she said, her voice unsteady.

Arni forgot all about the cucumber soup. What was it his father had said about Bielostrov? Had yet another war broken out there? Arni knew, of course, that a big war had started when he was quite small, that down in the south the Russians had killed their Tsar and that fighting was going on all over their country, but all those were such remote matters. Nothing had come near them at Raino where his father worked at Mr Pitoen's timber-yard; where he, Arni, went to the little school to learn sums, spelling and maps; where the small and lovely world of granite boulders, tall trees and running water had been his since he could remember. Now evidently something had happened to crash right across their lives. Arni moistened his lips.

'Father,' he ventured at last, 'what has happened?'

Nils tugged at the collar of his grey cotton shirt, then stroked his short fair beard. His grey eyes looked so unhappy that Arni did not dare to repeat his question.

'The frontier was closed last night,' Nils answered at last. 'The Russians stay on their side and we – on ours. They have got patrols out and they do terrible things to people they happen to catch. Mr Pitoen had large stocks of timber at Pargolovo and Oudelnaya, and those places are well behind the frontier. We live on the right side and nothing is likely to happen to us, but it is going to make things a bit hard.' He tried to smile at Arni. 'Never mind, son, we'll weather it all right.'

Arni stared.

'But what did you say about Bielostrov, Father?'

'That's where the frontier is,' Nils explained. 'It belongs to the Russians now. No more trips for us, son.'

Arni pushed his little bowl away.

'But what's to stop us?' he asked shakily. 'It is still near, isn't it?'

'What's to stop us? Why, guns and rifles. None of our people would like to be shot at.'

'But who has done it?'

'Closed the frontier, you mean? Why, the Russians. Finland is now a country on her own – and the Russians are in such a mess at home they are terrified of anyone peeping in, I suppose. So that's why they've closed the frontier.'

Arni sat dumb. His lovely secret . . . No more trips to Bielo-strov, no shops, no present for Kesti . . . All his efforts wasted . . . When Kesti tugged at his sleeve, he snapped at her, and Anna shook her head at him.

But Arni did not see this. Head bent, he jumped off the bench and ran out of the yard into the wood towards the river. There, on the flat mossy bank, his face against the hot grass, he cried, anger and disappointment like twin fangs biting deep and sharp into him. There, presently, Biki found him and licked the back of his neck, but Arni had nothing to say even to Biki. And there, some time later, his mother came. He had pushed Biki away. He could not do that to his mother, but he lay still, his hot swollen face turned away.

'Arni,' she said, her roughened hand stroking the tousled head. 'Arni!'

But he kept still. He could not cry any more. Nor could he speak.

'It is going to be pretty hard for everybody, son,' Anna went on, 'but it will be still harder if we start locking ourselves up from one another. There will be much less work for Father, your sheep-skin coat is going thin in places, and we might not be able to buy you a new one, but, at least, we shall be safe here at Raino, and perhaps we may move farther up north later on. God is good, Arni. Never forget that, will you? But don't lock yourself up, son. Now what is it?'

His face still turned away, Arni mumbled in a voice thick with unshed tears:

15

'Promise you won't tell, Mother, will you? It's been such a secret,' his shoulders shook, 'for Kesti's birthday.' Here Arni gulped hard, and his shattered plan came out in a few broken sentences.

'Now, now,' Anna said calmly, 'of course, I'll keep your secret and you'll keep your money. I can't find a box of coloured beads for you, but I've got a pretty new kerchief – a blue one with pink flowers all over it, and I don't think Kesti has ever seen it. You shall give that to her.'

'It won't be the same – '

'Of course not, but it is better than having no present at all, isn't it?'

Here Arni turned, lay on his back and stared at the deep blue cup of the June sky.

'Mother,' he began, 'it all seems such a muddle to me. Once a boy at Raino tore the hem off Kesti's pinafore, and I hit him, and he hit me back, and we had such a fight.'

'Yes, I remember. Your left ear was bleeding when you came in.'

'I hit him hard too,' said Arni, 'but it was just him and me. The other boys didn't meddle. I paid him out for Kesti's pinafore.'

'Well?'

Arni knit his forehead. He knew what he wanted to say, but words would not come to him. In his mind he saw a high spiked barrier stretched right across the road to Bielostrov and men with angry faces and loaded rifles guarding that barrier, and, as Arni saw it, there seemed no sense in any of it because nobody at Raino and in the neighbouring hamlets meant any harm to the people at Bielostrov. He remembered the plump, pink-cheeked old lady who kept the shop where he had hoped to buy the coloured beads. What had she to do with the closing of frontiers?

'Father's done no harm to the Russians,' he mumbled at last. 'Now he wants to go and fetch the timber, and they won't let him. It's all upside down, Mother.'

Anna sighed as she got up and smoothed out her crumpled red cotton skirt.

'Father will try and make it all clear to you, son, when you get a bit older. Now run and wash your face in the river and come back to the house. I'll show you the blue kerchief. Then there's that trestle you said you would mend for me. And have you done your sums for tomorrow?'

'It's so hot –'

'You get down to the sums, son, and you'll forget all about the heat.'

Arni scrambled to his feet and said, his eyes staring at the river:

'Mother, I am sorry. It was rude to run away from a meal, but I am a boy, and how could I cry with Kesti sitting there?'

Anna did not smile.

'Get down to your work, Arni, and you'll be a man indeed.'

CHAPTER 3

Another cloud in Arni's sky

Arni's way to school lay along the bank of the river, through a wood of fir, pine and larch, and across the wind-swept uplands sloping down to the village. It was a good two miles from his home, but he loved every inch of the way. On the hottest summer day, the wood remained cool and fragrant. It was good to run, his tanned legs brushing against the bracken fronds, his grey eyes eager for the least sign of bird and beast. Red squirrel, stoat, badger, an occasional hare, blackbird, tit, chaffinch and sparrow, Arni loved them all, and on that Monday morning it seemed to him a perfect world except for the stupidity of those who set up unnecessary barriers and made things harder for the people who

18

wanted nothing except to get on with their own work. He still thought about his shattered little 'secret'. He had seen the blue and pink kerchief, and he supposed that Kesti would like it. But it was not the same as that box of coloured beads he would never be able to buy.

The school, a low-roofed, pale timbered building, stood at the very edge of Raino. Its grounds fringed with thick lilac bushes, it had a pretty little garden in front. That morning, all its windows were flung wide open. It seemed a friendly place, and Arni was very fond of the teacher, who was gentle and patient, and brought excitement into every lesson – except arithmetic.

After prayers, the teacher left her desk and stood facing them, a small slight woman in dark blue, and at once they missed her smile. She looked grave. Her voice was almost solemn. Arni leant forward to listen to what she had to say, gripping the edge of his desk. It proved to be the same story about the closing of the frontier. She hoped they would all be careful and not wander too near the boundary because those were rather uncertain days. Then she said:

'Now Christmas is still some months ahead, children, but I am afraid that this year we shan't be able to have our tree. The Baroness's Wood is on the other side of the frontier and, as you know, we have no suitable trees in the neighbourhood. Of course, we'll have the usual party. Let's hope that things will have been settled in some way or other by next year.'

The teacher finished speaking and turned to her desk. A subdued whimpering broke out among the girls. Some of the boys muttered under their breath. But Arni sat very still.

What did his silly little 'secret' matter now? How could they have Christmas without a proper tree? It was impossible. The little tree with the gold star at the top which brought the three kings from the East into the house where the Child was waiting for them! How could the Child come into the house unless a tree were there to welcome Him? Arni's mother had often enough tried to make him see that the Child's coming did not depend on a decorated and lighted tree standing in the room, but Arni could never accept this. And he knew that Kesti never would. And now because of those unkind people on the other side of the barrier, they would miss the golden moment of the year when they sang of the Child's coming as the first tiny candle broke into flower. They could not very well fix those small painted candlesticks against the wall. It would never be the same. They were just painted candlesticks, and a tree was a living thing ... Arni was clenching his cold fists under the desk when his neighbour pushed him hard.

'Wake up! The teacher has been calling you.'

Arni got up rather shakily. He felt dazed. He looked at the teacher as though he did not see her. His hands were very cold.

'Arni,' said the teacher for the third time. 'Are you feeling ill?'

He shook his head. He remembered that on Mondays the first lesson was geography. He used to love it. Now he hated it.

'What river does London stand on?' she asked him.

Arni knew perfectly well, but he could not remember. He remembered nothing that morning. He stood there, biting his lips. From behind someone's voice whispered urgently: 'The Thames, the Thames,' and the teacher shook her head.

'No cheating, please. Arni, come to the blackboard and we'll try the map.'

That great map at Arni's school had been a most happy idea of the teacher's. It was a map of Europe, and when they first saw it, it had not got a single place-name on it. When any of them pointed correctly at a town, a river, or a mountain, they wrote the name underneath, with their own name following it. The teacher said that whoever got the greatest number of right answers would receive a fine picture-book as a prize. Arni was second in the running, with twelve names to his credit. Niki, a boy of ten, had fourteen, and Arni was determined to beat Niki.

'Now,' the teacher said, glancing at the map, 'where are the Orkneys?'

It should have been so easy, and it would have been on an ordinary morning. But, his world shattered, Arni could not gather his wits. He stood, the slim long stick upraised in his right hand. A moment later, the point of the stick brushed against the Channel Islands.

'Arni,' the teacher sighed, 'you must be feeling ill.'

'No, Teacher,' he mumbled, conscious of the blood mounting to his face. Whatever happened, it must never be said that he cried at school, and he wanted to cry most terribly.

'Let's try again,' said the teacher. 'Shall we go to Sicily?'

But it was no good: Arni placed Sicily at the southern tip of Spain. The teacher shook her head more in sadness than in anger, and said that Arni did not try hard enough. At the end of the lesson Niki's record stood at sixteen points, but Arni was past caring about the geography prize. During break he kept to himself in a corner of the garden. It bewildered him that the rest of them did not seem to care. Assured of their Christmas party and presents, they did not mind about the tree.

'But Mother will understand,' Arni kept reminding himself.

Yet everything went wrong that day. When he got home, he saw his mother in the doorway, a big basket on her arm and a pink striped kerchief over her head. She said she had been waiting for him to get back. She must go and do some sewing for a neighbouring farmer's wife, and Arni could take Kesti into the wood.

'Don't forget the baskets,' Anna added. 'Wood strawberries are at their best just now.'

She smiled and went. Arni stared angrily after her. In a corner of the little yard, under the limes, Kesti sat on the ground, putting a green print bonnet on her doll's head.

'Didn't you hear what Mother said?' Arni spoke gruffly. 'Come along!'

'I'll come if we take Titi,' Kesti replied.

'Of course not. Where's the sense of taking a doll into the wood?'

Kesti's blue eyes welled with tears.

'Titi isn't a doll. Titi – is Titi.'

Arni looked at the rag doll and knew he loathed it. It was so ugly, and in his opinion it was fit for a bonfire or the river.

'Come on,' he said and pulled Kesti up. The bonnet fell off the doll's head, and Kesti burst into tears.

'I want Titi to come – '

'All right, all right, bring it along, and stop snivelling, you're a big girl now.'

22

'Biki must come too,' Kesti announced, wiping off her tears. 'Please, Arni! It's such a hot day and the wood is so far. I could ride Biki.'

'You're much too big to ride him now. He'll stay behind and mind the chickens. A fox might come and ravage them, and you would never see another egg again. You wouldn't like that, would you?'

'No,' agreed Kesti. She clasped the doll in her arms, and trotted off by Arni's side.

He knew that he would have to keep an eye on her once they got into the wood. First, Kesti ate almost as many strawberries as she picked. Next, she never remembered the lesson he had taught her long ago: to leave at least one berry on every clump.

And it happened again that day. No sooner had Kesti seen a thick clump of wood strawberries than she ran, dropped her doll, and began picking and eating. Arni got angry with himself – he should never have taken his eyes off her.

'Can't you ever remember what I tell you? You must always leave one berry for the little people. They use wood strawberries for their shoe buttons. They get angry if they can't find any. I did tell you that they run about so much that they always lose their shoe buttons.'

Kesti listened, her pink-stained mouth opened wide.

'Have you seen them?'

'Whom?'

'Why, the little people – '

'I may have done,' Arni answered evasively, 'but they are very small – it is easy to miss them.'

'Smaller than Titi?'

'Smaller than your little finger, you silly.'

'I see,' said Kesti. 'Arni, I would like to keep some berries till winter comes.'

'Whatever for?'

'Till Christmas,' Kesti said pensively, 'when the tree is in the house, and I'll give the strawberries to the Child with the candles and everything.'

Arni turned his face away.

'They'd never keep till Christmas, and you know it.'

'I wish they would. You once said that the Child made everything. So He must have made the strawberries, and I'd like to see them on the tree. I wish He came in the summer,' said Kesti. 'There are no flowers or pretty berries to give Him in the winter – nothing but moss, and it is so cold.'

Arni flung himself on the ground.

'You are a silly,' he snapped. 'The Child could come into the house without any berries or a tree.'

Kesti shook her head.

'Never, Arni! He comes with the tree. I shut my eyes then because I want to see Him better. He never cries. He smiles. And we all sing, and the candles burn, and nobody is cross, and you never pull my hair because of the Child being there.' Kesti sighed deeply. 'I wish it were Christmas all the time. It is all so lovely, and Titi loves it too.'

Arni stared at his half-filled basket, his mouth set. Whatever could have put all those things into Kesti's head?

'Do you mean to tell me that the Child would not come if there were no tree?'

'Of course not,' Kesti's eyes opened wide in astonishment. 'People don't come unless they are asked, Mother said so, and the tree asks Him as soon as the star is there and the candles are lit. Arni, you know that, don't you?'

His bare legs tickled by the silken moss, Arni lay and did not answer. Kesti picked up the rag doll and began talking to it.

'Titi knows that when the Child is in the house, even Biki doesn't bark, and everything is so lovely because He is there, and He has made everything, you and me, and Father and Mother, and Biki and Titi. Of course, the tree must be there for Him.'

Arni stirred. It was cool and shady in the wood, and fragrant, too, because of the pine needles carpeting the ground. He lay on his back, and saw the sunlight ripple through the fir fronds. He heard the music of the little waterfall where the brook joined the river. A red squirrel leapt from one larch bough to another, his coat almost golden in the sun, and he saw a ladybird move across his toes. He lay very still. Then he said:

'Of course, you are right, Kesti. The tree must be there.'

And he could have bitten his tongue out as soon as he had said it. There would be no tree. There could not be, but he knew that to say so to Kesti would be far worse than hitting her. Arni leapt to his feet.

'Come on,' he said gruffly, 'Christmas is a good long way off. Look, your basket's nearly empty. Don't you go on gobbling up all the berries you find.'

At last, in spite of Kesti's greed, the baskets were filled with the tiny scarlet berries, and both of them left the wood for the river bank. Far ahead, through a clearing in the trees, they could see the pointed grey roof of their home. The little river looped and twisted, its banks enamelled with red and pink mosses, wild orchids, oxlip and watermint. Every so often Kesti would stop and say that she must pick some flowers, but Arni kept telling her that their baskets were too full.

Then Kesti stopped once again.

'Oh look, there's a boy fishing!'

Arni raised his head. Of all the people he had no wish to meet!

It was Niki, and Arni said:

'We'll get home quicker through the thicket. Come on.'

But Kesti would not leave the river bank. She said there were too many nettles in the thicket, and when Arni tried to pull her away from the bank, she cried so loudly that Niki heard, pulled up his line, and ran towards them.

'Nothing will bite,' he shouted, 'but I am four points above you for the geography prize, Arni, and that's something.'

'I'll beat you yet,' Arni scowled.

'That's what you think!'

'Come on, Kesti,' Arni turned away, when to his disgust his sister said politely:

'Would you like some strawberries? But you mustn't take too many – they are for Mother,' she paused and added, 'I wish there were strawberries in the winter. They'd look so pretty on the tree.'

'You – silly,' laughed Niki, 'who would ever think of hanging

26

berries on a Christmas tree? Anyway, you won't have one this year. Didn't you know that?'

Arni clenched his fists and stepped forward, his eyes flaming. And then he realized that he must not fight Niki. Kesti might think there was something in what he had said. Kesti, Arni said to himself, must never know.

Kesti stood, staring hard. Then she stamped her tiny bare foot and said calmly:

'You are not clever enough to catch fish. You are not clever at all. You are talking nonsense. Of course, the tree will be there. Arni said so, and Arni knows. He is clever. He's mended Mother's trestle. Arni is clever,' she repeated the words as though they were a challenge, clutching her doll tighter, and tilting the basket hanging on her arm. At once a scatter of berries fell on the yellow-green stubble, and Niki burst into loud laughter.

'You silly little girl! What's a trestle got to do with the Christmas tree? There won't be one, I tell you. And look at your strawberries! More than half of them gone!' he leapt forward and trampled them into the ground. For a second Kesti's eyes stared unseeingly at the crimson-veined grass. Then she let the basket fall on the ground and sobbed.

Arni sprang. Those wantonly crushed berries gave him a chance he had been longing for. Niki was two years older than him and much heavier. Arni was all hardened, supple muscle and bone, and he had fought bigger boys than Niki. Now, enraged by the other's stupidity and unkindness, Arni fought as he had never fought before. In a few minutes, Niki, his chin and temple bruised, his smock torn at the throat, and his left cheek swelling,

27

lay flat on the hot bruised grass, Arni's tanned foot on his chest, and begged for mercy.

'Ah,' panted Arni. 'Had enough, have you? Pick up the basket,' he ordered, 'and run into the wood and get more strawberries, and bring the basket back to my home, do you hear?' He moved his foot away, watched Niki stumble away towards the wood, and then turned to Kesti. 'Goodness, what are you crying for? Nobody's hurt you.'

'Titi is frightened,' Kesti sobbed. 'Please don't hit Titi.'

'I'll drown your beastly doll some day,' he said and flung himself down on the grass. Could Kesti ever understand? He loved her so much that he felt he could do anything for her, but she was such a nuisance. He had fought Niki for her, and she thought of nothing except her stupid doll.

Then a very sticky hot hand began pulling at his sleeve. Arni did not move.

'Please, I did not mean it. You'd never hurt Titi, I know –'

Arni said nothing. The little hand tugged harder and harder.

'And that boy told lies, didn't he? It's all nonsense – the tree will be there, Arni, won't it?'

He wished dumbly that he might shake Kesti's hand off his arm.

'Arni, he was lying, wasn't he?'

Arni spoke through clenched teeth:

'Yes, he was. Of course, the tree'll be there. Stop pulling at me, Kesti, and mind, say nothing about this to anyone at home – not even to Mother.'

'Yes, Arni, and Titi won't tell either.'

'Shut up,' said Arni.

They went home, Kesti absorbed in her doll and Arni troubled by the promise he knew he could never keep. The Baroness's Wood was in the hands of enemies. He had fought and beaten Niki. He knew he could never fight grown-up men – he must wait a long, long time before he was fit to do so, but Christmas would not wait. Christmas would come at the appointed time whatever people did or did not do.

They came to the little coppice near their home where the brook ran singing its little silver song, its banks fringed with larch and fir and elm. Arni had loved those trees all his life. That June afternoon he almost hated them. Why should those trees have grown so big? Why didn't they have a single small, properly-shaped *yelka* in the neighbourhood? The smallest fir in the coppice stood well over twenty feet, its branches starting somewhere half-way up the trunk.

In spite of his victory over Niki, Arni thought that life was a very difficult business.

CHAPTER 4

Shadows at home

In the days that followed Arni had little, if any, leisure to brood over the promise he had given so rashly.

Nothing was wrong with the world as he saw it. The perfect summer reached its height. The hay harvest was in, and its fragrance lingered over the fields. Now the corn was thickening and July brought an abundance of mushrooms and wild berries of all kinds. In all the orchards, trees bent low under their generous load of ripening fruit. People said that it would be an apple and pear year to remember for a long time. At every farmstead in the neighbourhood life hummed busily from before dawn till long after sunset.

But things were not particularly merry under Arni's home-roof. They had their faithful Kuki, the cow, Pengi, the old pony, some poultry, and a small kitchen garden, but they were not farmers. Timber was Nils's business, and had always been. Now many of Mr Pitoen's commitments lay south of the recently settled frontier between Finland and Russia. The frontier remained closed, and Mr Pitoen realized that, if things continued like this, he might well be a ruined man. He began paying his hands off one by one, and he was not certain how long he would be able to keep Nils. From six full days' work a week, Nils came down to four, three, and finally two. There was just not enough work at the timber-yard.

Nils knew it well. He tried to find some job at one or other of the neighbouring farms. Farmers were kindly enough people, but there were just no jobs going for a man who had never worked on a farm. Nils did not despair. He knew as well as everybody else that those were very difficult days for Finland. Trouble of one kind or another kept breaking out to the north and the east, and nobody could really tell if the civil war then clutching the whole of Russia in its violent grip would not end by engulfing Finland. Things were unsettled up and down in the country. Prices rose, and even some quite ordinary things could not always be had. Money was getting scarce.

Arni heard talk of all this at Raino. There was not much said by his parents at home, but he watched narrowly. Things were certainly getting grim. When the last spoonful of sugar was gone,

Anna bought no more. She reminded the children that they had plenty of honey. Kesti complained that Titi liked sugar better than honey, and Arni smacked her. Anna was angry.

'Say at once that you are sorry.'

He mumbled something under his breath. He did not feel a bit sorry. He, too, preferred sugar to honey, but he had not said so. Yet, when Kesti stopped crying, he tried to comfort her:

'I heard our teacher say the other day that sugar is bad for you. It does something or other to your teeth, she said. And things aren't as bad as all that, Kesti. We've still got Kuki. We'll never go short of milk.'

But there seemed little to comfort them as Arni saw it. He watched his mother spend hours mending his sheepskin coat which was almost past mending. He heard her say that he must be careful and not climb too many trees so as not to tear his one and only pair of leather breeches. He saw her go into the tiny larder, a frown on her face. When the last piece of bacon was eaten, she did not buy another flitch, and Arni knew that his mother had cried when the potato crop came up black and shrivelled with blight.

Summer slipped into autumn. The wind from the east beat sharp and cold into his face when Arni ran to the well in the early mornings. Berries were being formed on the holly and the bracken was turning bronze. Days grew shorter and shorter and soon, according to custom, school ended at noon.

Now Arni had to stay at home quite a lot; his mother was away so much, washing, sewing and mending at some of the farms. But nobody could afford to pay much, and there was never enough money. There were days when Arni knew that Anna went to the little market at Raino, a carefully tied-up bundle under her arm. She came back, sad and tired. She brought salt, candles, cotton thread, matches, and sometimes a little coffee.

Arnie well knew what those bundles contained. There was little enough to sell under their roof, and the things went one by one: the red and green embroidered counterpane from his parents' bed, a beautifully carved box of some pale foreign wood his father had once brought from Helsinki, a pair of heavy brass candlesticks . . . One by one, the treasures Arni had known all his life vanished from the little house.

Soon there came evenings when they sat down to none too well filled bowls of thin gruel for supper. Nils, the brief grace said, would rub his hands and say cheerfully:

'Never mind, children, we'll weather it in the end. Let's be thankful that we've not been hungry yet – '

Arni, his supper finished, knew he could have eaten twice as much. It was difficult to try and pretend that food did not matter. He did not try, and the smile would go off Nils's face and Anna's mouth would shake slightly. She knew well – even without Arni saying so – that he was still hungry, and she longed to see his little bowl refilled, but she knew she could not give him any more without using what food there remained for next morning's breakfast.

The house was warm enough; there was no lack of free fuel in the neighbourhood, and now that Nils had only two days' work in the week, he had ample time to fell trees and to saw the wood for the squat blue stove in the living-room. The stove had two

33

tiny doors in front. Often, in the evening, Anna would not have a candle lit; the doors stayed open, and they sat in the warm glowing light from the stove. Half-asleep, Arni dangled his legs from the trestle and dreamed of easier days to come, with the sadness gone from his mother's eyes, a well-filled sugar bowl on the table, and a new sheepskin coat on his shoulders.

CHAPTER 5

The day Arni got the geography prize

Meanwhile, whatever people did or did not do, the procession of the seasons continued. The first snow fell early enough, and Kuki, the cow, had to be fetched in for the night, and the little door into the hen-house made secure against the possible invasion of a hungry fox. In the early mornings, the whole country looked as if it were carved out of some shining white stone, veined here and there with blue, pink and silver. The snow fell quietly, caressingly, a friend to tree, shrub, grass and moss. All the winds in the world

35

seemed to have gone far, far away. In the wood not a twig of a larch but remained still.

Arni, as usual, was well prepared for the winter. The little sledge, covered with worn brown leather, the small skis, and the skates he often used for crossing the river, were all there. Within a week after the first snow-fall, he knew he could use his skis for the run to school. His father said:

'Yes, I should say there's enough snow – but mind you keep away from the river, son. The ice has not had time to settle yet.'

Arni loved skiing, and the first run was always a triumph. Even the meagre breakfast he had had could not damp down his pleasure. The world looked so clean and wonderful, and it was just impossible that anything really grim could happen to anyone. The wood was an enchanted, stilled enclosure. The ice across the brook was so delicate that he could see the dark green water running underneath, and that deepened the morning's loveliness for him. He whistled to every squirrel he saw and laughed at a hare scuttling away at his approach. It was pure joy to catch hold of a larch limb and feel the cold flakes scatter all over his face, head and shoulders.

Leaving the wood, Arni raced across the vast uplands and flashed like an arrow down the broad slope leading to the fringes of Raino. Only when he reached the school house, did he realize how early he was: not a boy nor a girl was to be seen anywhere. Arni stooped to unstrap the skis when he heard the teacher's voice calling to him from the back door.

'You are early! Just as well because I want to speak to you. Come in through the back door.'

Arni's heart gave a thump. Had he done anything? He could not remember. His work had not been particularly good. In fact, his sums had been very bad for weeks. But, surely, the teacher would not speak to him about sums before school began. His heart beating wildly, Arni ran to the back door. The teacher, her shoulders wrapped in a big grey shawl, stood waiting for him in the narrow passage. She was coughing as he opened the door, and her cheeks looked flushed, but she did not seem cross, and Arni breathed a little more easily.

'It is about the big map,' she said. 'How many points must you have to get the prize?'

The question surprised him.

'Why, twenty-one, Teacher.'

'And how many have you got?'

'Nineteen.'

'You top the list, I think?'

'Why, yes, Teacher.' And Arni added: 'Niki comes next. I scored two last week and that put me ahead of him.'

'Yes, I know.'

Arni's eyes opened wide. He could not understand why she was asking him all those questions. She knew the answers as well as he did. Why, it was only last week that 'Gibraltar' and 'Dublin' had raised his score to nineteen.

'Come with me,' she said a little abruptly. 'There is nobody in the schoolroom. It is just as well that you and I should be alone there.'

Wholly bewildered, Arni followed the teacher down the passage. The schoolroom was warm and empty. The teacher closed the door and crossed to the wall where the great map hung next to the blackboard.

'Look at the map,' she said in an oddly tautened voice, 'and tell me what you see there.'

Arni looked hard, and wondered if he had better rub his eyes. No, what he saw was clear enough: four place-names, written in his own hand, and four of his signatures were wiped off. Whoever had done it was not particularly clever. Some of the letters still showed, however faintly: the 'b' of 'Gibraltar', the 'r' of his own signature here and there, and the 'D' of 'Dublin' still stood out clearly.

'Well,' the teacher said at last, 'have you any idea who could have done it?'

Arni's face went scarlet and he bit his lip. He had a very good idea indeed. He remembered Niki saying the day before that he must stay behind after school and look for a pencil he had lost. Arni's ears were burning as he said:

'It was not me, Teacher.'

'Don't be silly, Arni, and answer my question.'

His eyes on the map, Arni replied stolidly:

'I've had fights with nearly all the boys here, Teacher, and – well – few of them have ever beaten me.'

'Is that an answer?'

'That's all I can tell you, Teacher,' Arni replied in the same wooden voice. Ah yes, he would get even with Niki. As soon as school was over, that very day, he would give Niki the thrashing of his life, but that was not a thing to be said to anyone, least of all to the teacher.

'Is that all, Arni?' she asked.

'Why, yes, Teacher.'

'Well, but there is something I am now going to tell you because of what you would not tell me. Someone was mean enough to try and cheat you of your prize. I know that you know who it is, but you needn't worry – I am not asking for any names. When school begins this morning, you shall put back those four place-names, and I have decided to hand you the prize today, you understand?'

Arni did not. He stared, his face burning a wild red. Then he faltered:

'But, Teacher, I had only nineteen points, not twenty-one.'

'Don't argue,' she broke in, 'and get to your desk. I can hear them coming.'

She turned and left the classroom. Arni went to his desk and cupped his burning face in both hands. Yes, it was Niki's revenge for the thrashing he had had in the summer. It was mean – and stupid too, but Arni could not see why the teacher should have decided to give the prize to him that very morning.

Soon enough the room rang with the thumping of feet and shrilly shouting voices. From his desk Arni watched Niki come in and dart an anxious glance at the great map. Then, suddenly reassured, he turned and his eyes met Arni's.

'Road good for skiing?' he asked.

'Fair.'

'I say, it's geography this morning, isn't it?'

'Yes –'

'You staying behind today? I thought that we might start building a snowman in the garden.'

'I'm wanted at home,' Arni said curtly.

'Tomorrow then?'

'I couldn't say.'

'Now what's come over you?' Niki began, when the teacher came in and they all got up.

After prayers, the teacher faced the children, and her eyes were grave.

'Something happened here after school yesterday, and I am deeply ashamed of it. I am not asking any questions, but I want you to know that someone tried to cheat Arni of his chances to win the geography prize. I asked him if he had any idea who that boy or girl might be, and Arni would not tell me. Nor do I want to know. As you remember, he was at the very top with nineteen points to his credit, and because of his loyalty to you all I have decided to give the prize to him this morning.'

A peony in full bloom might have looked dull by comparison with Arni's face. He stared at his boots and he stared at the ceiling. The room stirred. His particular friends became vocal in their anger and disgust, but the teacher at once raised her hand.

'I want none of you to start guessing. Nobody's to talk about it, do you hear? Arni, come here.'

Unsure, his hands shaking, Arni stumbled towards the teacher's desk. There, in its beautiful tooled binding, lay the coveted prize, an enormous book with coloured pictures of animals, birds, trees and flowers. They had already seen it on the teacher's desk soon after Easter holidays. Now it was to be his . . . Arni's hands shook so that he could hardly hold the heavy book. The cheering and clapping behind him served to deepen his confusion. The teacher smiled when Arni muttered his thanks. He turned back to his desk, raised his head and saw Niki there, in the middle of the room, fury all over his face, and at once a terrible fear flashed through Arni's mind.

The book was so heavy. He would never be able to ski back home, and it was clear that Niki was planning a revenge. Suppose that Niki gained on him, hid somewhere behind a tree, and then pounced . . . Niki would certainly get as good as he gave, but the precious book would just as certainly get damaged in the scuffle. He must, Arni thought wildly, leave the book safely behind for a few days and then ask his father to come down to Raino and fetch it. Almost in a daze, he turned back to the teacher's desk. He knew her to be fair and kind. He hoped she would understand.

'Please,' he mumbled, 'may I leave it with you for a day or two, Teacher?'

'Don't you want to take it home at once? Or is it too heavy for your satchel?' she asked and, then, as though she had indeed grasped the reason for Arni's sudden distress, she added briskly: 'Why, I understand – you couldn't ski back, could you? Well, as your home is so far, Arni, you may leave an hour sooner today and do your Scripture lesson at home. Is that all right?'

Too happy to speak, Arni nodded. Really, it seemed a day of miracles. He knew that the book would be safe enough in the classroom. Niki would never dare play any of his tricks till school was over and by that time he, Arni, would have his treasure safely at home.

The book carefully put into his satchel, the skis strapped to his back, he started for home just as the school clock boomed eleven. It was truly a magic day. The pale wintry sun was out, and the icy traceries on the small windows of Raino houses were like so many folds of jewelled lace. The village looked as though it had prepared itself for a high festival. Beyond the houses, tree and shrub wore their silver-white cloaks with grace and dignity. The icy-cold tang in the air caressed rather than menaced. The snow carpet was kind to his feet. The world seemed new, clean, and full of promise. It was a morning for singing and for laughter, and Arni's thoughts wandered far away from the sadness in his mother's eyes and the empty larder shelves at home. And even when he remembered the latter, he said to himself that never again would he ask for the second helping of gruel at supper.

Anna was busy at the stove when Arni rushed in, halted to thump the snow off his boots, and shouted:

'Mother, the prize, the prize! I've got it, I've got it –'

He almost forgot to close the door behind him – he was in such a hurry to undo the thongs of the satchel.

'Look! See the gold lettering! And hundreds of pictures – all in colour, too. Look at this gorgeous bird – all crimson and blue, and here is an almond tree in flower . . . Mother, isn't it lovely?'

Anna, wiping her hands on the pink-striped apron, smiled warmly. It was indeed good to have that much sunshine brought into the house.

'Splendid, son! What did you get it for?'

'Why, geography!'

She laughed.

'Well, I didn't think you would have got a prize for your sums. Now, run, little son, and put it away in your chest, and we'll have it out tonight when Father is here,' she stooped, kissed Arni's forehead, and whispered: 'I am proud of you.'

Arni had no room of his own. He slept on a small landing which opened out at the top of the short stairway. The landing had a window, and the tiny chest where he kept his few 'treasures' stood right underneath. At right angles to it was his little bed of planks with a flat straw mattress and a pillow stuffed with goose feathers. To the left was the door leading to the only bedroom of the house, where his parents slept with Kesti's cot at the foot of their bed. Opposite that door was a bigger chest where, as Arni knew, his mother kept her own 'treasures' and what little house-linen they had.

He found a clean towel, wrapped up his prize, and put it into his chest. Then, turning towards the stairway he saw that an oblong wooden box stood on the top of his mother's chest. Arni did not have to look twice: that was the box where the Christmas tree ornaments were kept from one year to another. What did his mother mean by having it out? The box at once reminded Arni of his reckless promise to Kesti. It also filled him with unease. He came down the stairs at the double.

'Mother, why have you got the ornaments box out?'

Anna, bending over a saucepan, did not answer at once.

'I had no idea you would be back so early today. Is the teacher ill?'

'No, no,' he said impatiently. 'What do you want the ornaments out for, Mother? It's simply ages till Christmas – '

43

Anna sighed and went on stirring the stew.

'I wish you had not come back so early,' she said at last. 'Now you must promise not to tell Kesti. She's at the back somewhere playing with Biki.'

'Not to tell her what?'

'Well, it's market day at Raino tomorrow. I thought of giving all those things a good rub – '

'Mother, you are not going to sell them?'

Anna's voice shook a little.

'I had hoped to keep it all from you, son, but there's just nothing else left.'

Arni would not listen.

'You mustn't, you mustn't! They are not yours . . . They belong to us all . . . How could we ever have a tree without a star?'

'But there'll be no tree this year,' she reminded him, her own eyes full of tears, 'and things should be easier sooner or later. By the time next Christmas comes round, we might get another star – perhaps even a bigger and a brighter one.'

Arni was past listening.

'You mustn't, you mustn't, you mustn't – ' he kept repeating, tears cascading down his cheeks.

The box was still upstairs on the landing, but he could imagine its contents spread out on the square table in the living-room, each of them so familiar and so beloved: the great golden star, the twelve tiny candlesticks, shaped like foxglove petals, their metal painted violet, pink and crimson, the four streamers of silver and gold foil so carefully preserved from year to year, the six small balls of bright green and amber glass, a handful of gilt walnuts, the funny monkey, bear and horse made of cardboard covered with silver tinfoil, two tiny crimson sledges, their infinitesimal bells breaking into music whenever a twig was touched, and a few other odds and ends, all brightly coloured, all deeply cherished, all sharing a place with the old carols, the stories from the Bible, the Child's coming. Take such things to the market? It was unthinkable.

'Stop crying,' Anna spoke a little sharply. 'Kesti might be in any minute, and what will she think?'

But Arni sobbed on and on.

'Sell my book,' he gulped, 'that will fetch something.'

'Don't be silly! What would people say if they saw me bring my son's prize to the market?' Anna pulled the saucepan off the fire and added wearily: 'Go and wash your face. Say nothing to Kesti.' Anna hesitated, and added 'I'll talk to Father this evening. I might not go to Raino after all.'

Arni raised his swollen, red-mottled face.

'Oh please don't,' he said brokenly, 'I'd do anything, Mother – chop wood, milk cows for neighbours . . . anything – I could earn quite a bit, I am so strong.'

Anna smiled and laid her hand on the tousled head.

'You've got your school work, son, and you help me quite a lot in the house. That's enough! Now run and wash your face. Anyone would think you'd had a thrashing.'

'I would never have cried for that,' Arni said and ran up the stairs.

CHAPTER 6

A promise must be kept

In the end, the oblong wooden box went back into the chest, its contents undisturbed, and Anna did not again talk about going to Raino. The glittering glories of the Christmas tree were safe, but Arni knew little peace.

More than ever did he realize that – come what might – it was his duty to bring the tree into the house. But where was he to look for one? He knew there were trains running westwards from Raino, and he supposed there were many other places like the Baroness's Wood with trees of the exact shape and size for the Child's birthday, but where were such woods, and how could anyone plan a journey when they did not really know where to go, and when they had no money for the fare? Except for his one trip to Helsinki, Arni had never travelled beyond Raino. All the excursions he had ever made had been to the south-east, to Bielostrov now so cruelly and wholly beyond his reach.

Even if, by making careful inquiries, Arni came to hear of a likely place, he had no money for the fare. He still had the small sum he had saved for Kesti's birthday, but he had enough sense to realize that even a short journey by rail would cost much more than that.

And there was something else too. It worried Arni that nobody seemed to show much concern about the Baroness's Wood being on the wrong side of the frontier. He thought of it a great deal, and it seemed to him that the coming Christmas was particularly important – things were in a pretty mess all round and the Child's help was needed more than ever, and yet everybody seemed indifferent. At school, they joined in the prayers and sang the hymns as loudly as ever, but Christmas to them meant little more than a solid meal and a few presents.

Arni added an artless petition to his evening prayers:

'Everything was made by You, and You can do everything. Please make it possible for me to bring Your tree into the house, dear, beautiful Child.'

That promise so recklessly given to Kesti was the greatest 'secret' Arni had ever had. Generally, all his 'secrets' were as warm and exciting as a good log fire on a cold wintry night. But this 'secret' was different. It did not warm him at all. It was like a fang biting deep and sharp. And it mocked at him, too, turning him into a silly little braggart of a boy.

'But I did not brag,' Arni would try and argue with himself. 'I meant to do it, and I mean to do it still. And I must start planning for it. The first thing to do is to make the stand for the tree.'

In winter, the only private nook Arni had was his tiny summer house. Unheated and draughty, it was avoided by Kesti who said that her Titi would die of cold if she went there. His parents never came near it at all. Arni knew that he would not dare to light a candle there. Daylight hours grew shorter and shorter, and an hour or so on Sunday mornings was all he could really count on.

He found two pieces of lime-wood in a corner of the shed. He had often watched his father make such stands. They were easy enough. Two carefully measured pieces of wood were planed and joined together to form a cross. Arni had the hammer and the thin long nails needed for the job. The next thing was to hollow out the middle of the joined planks so that the tree would stand firm and not wobble. For that Arni had a knife given him by Nils on his seventh birthday. He never took that knife to school for fear of losing it. It was a beautiful knife, sheathed in stout red leather, and it had six blades. Arni kept it at the bottom of his little chest.

The wood, the hammer and the nails were already smuggled into the summer house. One very cold Sunday morning Arni slipped upstairs, opened the lid of the chest, and lifted his prize book. The knife would be at the bottom, close to his fishing-tackle.

But he could not see it. He rummaged all over the chest. The knife had gone. He squatted in front of the chest and tried to remember when he had had it out last, but he could not remember. He went down the stairs. His parents were out. By the stove Kesti sat on a low stool, combing her doll's frizzed hair with the remnant of a comb.

48

'Much too cold for Titi to walk,' she said conversationally, and Arni looked at her hard, suspicion in his eyes.

'Seen my knife anywhere, have you?'

Kesti's fat little chin shook a little. She went on pushing the comb in and out.

'Kesti – '

Her underlip trembled. Her eyes were pools of confusion, fear and remorse.

'Arni, I looked and Titi looked, and even Biki looked, and we all looked so hard – '

'So you took it then,' Arni broke in, his voice slurred with anger, 'after I'd told you never to touch it. What would you say if I threw your beastly doll away, tell me that?'

'But I did not throw the knife away, Arni,' she protested. 'It fell – you know – the way things fall. Titi and I were cutting twigs, and the knife fell, and we looked and we looked – '

'Where?' he broke in.

'Oh not very far, Titi can't walk far.'

'Was it to the back of the house or in front?'

Kesti shook her head. She could not remember. Nor could she tell him when it had happened. 'The sun was warm, and we went for a walk,' she added helpfully.

'Was it before the snow?.

'Oh yes, long before,' Kesti replied. 'And Titi is sorry, Arni.' She stopped struggling with the tangled yellow curls and offered him the broken comb. 'Titi says she would like you to have this instead.'

That was more than Arni could bear. He snatched at the comb, broke it tooth by tooth, threw the pieces on the floor and stamped hard on them in a fury of rage.

'Oh Arni . . . Titi wanted you to have it. Now she is unhappy. She is crying.'

'Be quiet,' Arni shouted. 'You – little fool – taking my knife and losing it and never saying a word. I've fought and fought for you, but next time any boy teases you, I'll let him do it, see if I don't.'

'I am sorry . . . Titi is sorry . . .' Kesti cried, but Arni was at the door, and slammed it so hard as he went out that everything rattled on the dresser shelves.

In the little yard he stood and looked about. He knew it would be useless to try and find the knife. Kesti, who always complained of being tired whenever he took her for a walk, could wander quite a distance by herself especially when she had Biki with her. That precious, beautiful knife might have been lost on the uplands, or in the fir coppice, or in the great thicket of shrub and thorn at the back of the house. Before the snow, she had said. It would have gone rusty by now, Arni thought bitterly.

It was several minutes before he could trust himself to go back to the house. In the living-room, Kesti, kneeling on the floor, was trying to scoop up the broken fragments of the comb. Tears were still running down her plump pink cheeks.

'Kesti,' Arni swallowed hard, 'I am sorry, I did not mean it. If anyone were to tease or hurt you, I'd fight them just the same, you understand?' and he stooped, gathered up the bits and pieces of the comb, threw them away, and came back to kiss Kesti's wet cheek.

'You said the tree would come,' she said, her head bent, 'and

50

I'll ask the Child to give you another knife. I am sorry, Arni.'

For an answer he leapt up the stairs, and soon came down, the prize book in his arms.

'Keep your hands off it,' he ordered, 'and I'll show you some of the pictures.'

CHAPTER 7

A strange day at school

The market at Raino was held in the middle of the week, and on that morning Arni slipped out of the house much earlier than usual. All the money he had, counted and re-counted several times, lay in a small blue purse at the bottom of his satchel. Arni had no idea if the sum was enough to pay for a knife, but he knew that a knife he must have. Once the little stand was made, he would start 'exploring' in earnest.

The market opened some time before he was due at school. He ran into the wide street, and he saw bunches of people standing here and there and talking, but he took no notice of them. There were so many people at Raino, and they always bunched together and talked. Arni got to the very end of the street where it opened out into an irregular square, and for about twenty minutes he wandered from stall to stall. What use to him were pieces of crockery and saucepans, reels of black and white cotton, balls of thick string, cattle medicines, hairpins, bags of dried mushrooms and boxes of raisins? Never, Arni thought, did the market seem so dull as on that morning when, for the very first time, he was there with money in his pockets.

Even the weather heightened his disappointment. The skies were now shrouded in thick woollen grey, and presently flakes of wet snow began falling. It was almost time for school when, at the very last stall, Arni saw some pencils, a white porcelain ink-stand, its lid badly chipped, and a beautiful knife sheathed in faded crimson leather. Arni, his eyes starry, asked, trying to keep the excitement out of his voice:

'How much, please?'

The bent-shouldered stall-holder, muffled up to his nose in scarves and shawls, saw a small shabby schoolboy and shrugged, but his voice was not unkind. Arni was by no means sure that he had enough money. Fingers all numb, he fumbled with the thongs of his satchel until the man all but lost his patience.

'Here, snow is coming, and I want to be off. Do you want the knife, or don't you?'

'Oh please,' Arni begged, undoing the satchel at last, and pulling out the little blue purse. He had enough money – to the man's surprise and his own.

'Mind you don't play with those blades – they are very sharp,' the man warned him. 'Off to school, are you? Well, God bless you, little man, for you'll get no schooling today. What hard days, dear goodness, what hard days these are.'

Arni stared. What was the man talking about? No schooling

53

that day? Yet the familiar bell was pealing down the street, and Arni ran, the knife safe in his satchel.

The courtyard outside the school was crowded – but not with children. Men and women stared at Arni as he ran in, and everything seemed in such confusion that he could hardly find his way to the door. Once inside the little hall, he ran into one of the older girls who gripped him by the arm.

'Arni, there'll be no school today. The teacher's dead.'

He stared angrily.

'What in the world are you talking about? She was well enough yesterday.'

'She has not been well for ages,' said the girl. 'Her dreadful cough! She was taken ill yesterday afternoon and died in the evening. Now the inspector from Valparu is coming.'

'What for?'

'I don't know. Perhaps, to give us a lesson, or to tell us there'll be no school.'

'But who told you about the teacher?' Arni asked.

'Why, the whole of Raino knows. My sister heard it at the shop early this morning. They say the teacher's heart stopped. She used to cough such a lot, didn't she?'

'But nobody dies because of a cough,' said Arni.

The girl had no more time to spare for him and went off, with a shrug.

Arni wandered along to the classroom. They were all there, and all were quiet. But he still did not quite believe it. It seemed about as possible as to imagine snow falling down on summer roses. Arni's throat hurt him a little, because he must keep back his tears. The teacher had always been kind, fair, and so patient. Now he remembered all the occasions when his appallingly muddled sums, or the smudged state of his exercise-book, or his stubbornness in insisting that Portugal was an island, oh so many things, must have grieved her. She had scolded him often enough, but her manner of doing so had never been harsh. Arni turned to the nearest window and dug his fists into his eyes.

'I wish,' he thought, 'that I had told her about Kesti and the tree. She would have understood. She might have helped.'

The door opened. In came, not the inspector from Valparu with his long white beard, which always scared them, but the inspector's wife, whom they did not know at all. She had taken off her coat and shawls, and stood there, a plump red-cheeked woman in a bright green woollen dress, with a huge silver brooch at her throat. She ran rather than walked up to the desk, clapping her podgy hands, and Arni disliked her on sight.

'Good morning, my dear children,' she began in a thickly buttered voice. 'You have all heard the sad news, haven't you? There is to be no school today, and when you go home, you must tell your dear parents that there will be no school for two or three weeks until we have found some very nice lady to come here to teach you. But you will all understand,' she went on, her bright brown eyes sweeping over the room, 'that today is not a real holiday and you must not be idle at home. Go over your sums and other things, and be very, very good. I am sure you will be. I am just going to say prayers and then ask you a few questions from the Scriptures. All quiet now, children.'

The room was quiet enough, but a tumult was going on in

Arni's mind. If 'the very nice lady' was going to be the same as this woman with the sugary voice who said such silly things, he, Arni, would never come to school again. What did she think they all were – babies just out of their cradles?

'Now,' the inspector's wife said briskly, 'I am afraid I don't know your names,' she paused and smiled engagingly, but nobody returned the smile, and a plump pink forefinger singled out Niki. 'Tell me, dear child, what was the name of the first man?'

A subdued gasp rippled all over the room. Did the lady imagine they had never done any Scripture?

'Adam,' Niki replied a little sullenly.

'Splendid! Good boy!' the inspector's wife clapped her hands and looked at the girl seated just in front of Arni.

'Now, my dear little girl, what is the name of the book where we read all about Adam?'

'Why, the Bible, Teacher.'

'Splendid again, but, my little one, you mustn't call me that. I am Mrs Nillson.'

'The Bible, Mrs Nillson,' the girl said stolidly, and something like a smothered titter broke out here and there. The inspector's wife shook her head.

'Now, now, we mustn't be naughty today, we mustn't indeed. It is a very sad day for us all, and we must be very, very good.' Here her sharp eyes fell on Arni. 'My dear boy, tell me the name of Adam's wife?'

'Maria,' answered Arni, his face expressionless.

'Oh surely, you couldn't have forgotten? Try again, dear child. It's such a short and simple name. Now then – '

'Rebecca,' offered Arni in the same wooden voice.

'The name is Eve,' Mrs Nillson said reprovingly. 'Small as you are, you should have known that, dear boy.'

Arni did not reply. He sat down and exchanged glances with his neighbour, Erni, the blacksmith's son, sometimes a friend, sometimes an enemy. That morning Erni's grey eyes shone with admiration, and he followed in Arni's steps by telling the inspector's wife that Moses was found in Noah's ark.

Somehow Mrs Nillson did not ask many questions after that. She looked about, fingered her silver brooch, reminded them of 'the sad day' again and again, and hoped they would work hard at their studies at home. They were all wishing her gone when Arni got up suddenly.

'Please,' he stopped because he did not know what to call this strange woman, 'please, have you any Christmas trees at Valparu?'

The inspector's wife looked horrified.

'What a question to ask on such a day,' she gasped, 'and you did not know the name of Adam's wife! I don't suppose you know what Christmas is?'

Arni kept silent. He felt she did not expect him to answer. She gave him a glance which would have frozen a running stream in June, and then her eyes travelled up and down the room.

'I very much hope that the nice lady who will be coming here will correct all these gaps, children. I must say I feel disappointed.'

They kept very quiet and soon it was over. The plump pink hands, the bright green dress and the silver brooch all vanished, and they watched her go with deep relief in their hearts. Niki edged nearer to Arni's desk.

'Want a Christmas tree, do you? Nothing is easier. Take a train and make for Helsinki. Just an eight-hour journey, and the market there is so full of them that if you stole one, nobody would notice.'

'Be quiet before I hit you,' Arni hissed back.

Presently, Erni and Arni were the only ones left in the school-room. Arni wished that Erni would go and leave him alone for a bit, but he did not like to say so.

'You and your Maria,' Erni teased him.

'And what about your Moses? You are a copy-cat.'

'Say that again!'

'I'm going to. You are a copy-cat!'

'Just you wait a moment,' Erni began, but Arni shook his head.

'Oh no, you won't, not here and not this morning.'

Erni unclenched his fists.

'I'll miss the teacher a lot, Arni.'

'She was all right.'

'And she liked you. Once when we were doing botany, you said some firs grew near your house that had such big cones that you saw one kill a bird as it fell. The teacher asked if you would bring some of them into school, and you promised. You remember? And later when you'd gone out, someone said you'd forget, and the teacher said no, you never forgot or broke a promise, and Niki was furious.'

'He would be,' Arni exclaimed. 'She said that, did she?'

'Yes, and it is true, isn't it?'

'How do I know?' Arni began putting his books and pencils into the satchel, and Erni scrambled off the bench.

'Oh dear, and I'd nearly forgotten. Next week is my birthday,

Arni, on Thursday. Will you come and eat with us? Mother said I was to ask you. There'll be plenty of boiled bacon, and my sister is good at making honey-cakes.'

'Thanks, I will,' and Arni blushed for pleasure: this was his first invitation to Erni's house.

Erni went. Arni knew it was time for him to go too. But he sat still, his chin propped in both hands The teacher had said that he kept his promises, and she was not there for him to tell her that he had given a promise he simply could not keep.

It was snowing hard by the time Arni got home. Biki met him just outside the yard, and Arni made for the summer house. It was bitterly cold and dark inside, and Arni hugged Biki tight. 'Biki, Biki, what am I to do now?' he muttered, his cheek pressed against the shaggy shoulder. 'I must keep that promise! Surely, I must . . .' Arni shivered, but not because of the snowflakes falling on his face and under his collar. The whole world was such a cold, dark place. At last he moved and made for the house. In the living-room, the doors of the big stove were open, and the glow of crackling logs lit up now one corner, now another. Arni saw his mother in the rocking chair, her knitting-needles glinting silver in the firelight. He stooped to pull off his snowboots and said:

'The teacher died last night, Mother.'

The needles falling into her lap, Anna looked up.

'God house her well! But how very sudden! I am sorry, son, I know you'll miss her.

Arni said nothing.

CHAPTER 8

The wonder of the discovery

He had a new knife. The stand for the tree was made and hidden under some rags in the summer house. Now Arni knew that he must start exploring the neighbourhood. He had plenty of time. His appointed jobs done, he could do what he liked. Anna would not have him idle, but so long as Arni kept busy, she seldom asked questions and never nagged.

Everything answered his purposes – except the weather.

For nearly a week the wind and the snow seemed to be in

league against him. Arni had to bend nearly double when he crossed the yard to give fodder to the animals and the hens. The roar of the wind was so deafening that they almost had to shout at one another inside the house. Nils lost a week's wage because it was impossible for him to get near the timber-yard. Even above the roar of the storm they kept hearing crashes as great trees fell in the wood beyond the brook, and every crash made Kesti cry that she felt sure the roof would fall in. There was no sun, the very sky seemed to have vanished behind a thick murkily grey blanket, and Arni's parents said they could never remember such a storm.

One morning they woke to find icy blasts rushing right through the little house. They came down to find the living-room thickly carpeted with wet snow. Three of the outer shutters had got loose from their hinges, and the wind, beating against the windows, had broken all the glass panes. Nils at once got his hammer and some nails, muffled himself up to his eyes, and went to repair the shutters. Arni slipped out behind his father. They stood with their backs to the wind, and even so it all but wrenched the hammer out of Nils's hands. After several attempts, he got one of the hinges back in its place – only to see it torn off within an instant.

'Go back, son,' he shouted in Arni's ear.

But Arni, his head muffled in thick shawls, would not go back. He felt he could be of some use there, handing the nails to Nils and then pressing his determined hands against the shutter whilst his father went on hammering.

At last one of the shutters was mended, but it was out of the question to struggle with the other two. Panting and gasping for breath, father and son managed to wrench the door open. Once inside, Nils fixed some rough planks to the broken windows to keep the snow out. In spite of the wide open stove doors, the room looked dim and grey, but Anna said that they could not waste their few candles by daylight.

'You cannot call this daylight, Mother,' grumbled Arni.

It was not a kind thing to say, but he did not feel kind. When he heard his father tell Anna of his fears that the storm might continue right into the New Year, Arni's heart all but missed a beat. Could it mean that God was punishing him for a promise he should never have made? Arni's anxiety rose to a pitch, and he could not confide his anguish even to Biki. All of them were now huddled together in the living-room, there was not a shadow of a chance to run out into the garden and take refuge in the summer house, which was all but buried in a snowdrift. So Arni was depressed and kept snapping at Kesti until Nils cuffed him and threatened him with a beating unless he mended his manners.

After nearly a week, the storm died down. Waking up one morning, Arni breathed hard on his small window. It was still dark, but he could see the stars in the sky. He lay back and listened. All he heard was Kuki mooing in her stall. He crept out of bed and groped towards his parents' door.

'Kesti,' his whispered urgently, 'are you awake?'

'Yes,' came a very sleepy voice. 'What is it? Has the roof fallen in?'

'Silly!' Arni spoke affectionately. 'The storm is over. Everything's quiet.'

'Take Titi for a walk then,' mumbled Kesti comfortably and fell asleep again.

But Arni scrambled into his clothes, ran downstairs, and opened the door. The frost kissed his forehead and cheeks. He stood, sniffing hungrily. The world seemed stilled indeed. No more snow had fallen during the night. That much he could see. He raised his head. Yes, there were the stars, God's stars come back to comfort and reassure him. And how good it was to drink in the pure cold air without having his breath all but beaten out of him!

Arni closed the door softly and became busier than he had been for days. He fed more logs into the stove, set the pan of porridge on the fire, tiptoed to the dresser for mugs and plates, set the table for breakfast, and swept the room. Then he got into his sheepskins, muffled his head in a scarf, seized a pail, and ran across the yard to Kuki's stall, careful not to let his lantern go out. Kuki met him with a plaintive moo. 'But I am not too late, old girl,' Arni said as he seized the little stool, and set the pail down. The silken swish of the milk was like singing to him. He felt as though he were standing at the threshold of his great adventure. It was bound to come. It would come. He remembered that it was Sunday, and Christmas Eve fell on the following Friday.

After breakfast, Nils at once left for the timber-yard, and Arni, all his chores finished, said he would like to go for a good long tramp. Anna did not object.

'Mind you don't tumble into a snowdrift,' was all she said, 'and if I were you, I would not take Biki today. I don't want Kesti to go out and he will be company for her.'

Wisely, Arni left his skis behind. He knew that the gale would have swept the snow away in many places. He wore his big

63

snowboots, and he managed to slip a couple of rye rusks into the pocket of his sheepskins.

Once over the brook, he halted. He knew it would be no use his going westwards to Raino or even beyond it. He must turn eastwards. He marched off, taking deep breaths of the pure cold air. The going was not particularly easy – so many uprooted trees lay across his path, and Arni had to scramble across them and take great care not to tear his clothes. But at last the great wood lay behind him, and he found himself on the eastern edge of the uplands, not a tree, not a shrub to be seen anywhere. The snow lay thin on the ground, and here and there it had been swept clean off, and icy patches glinted in the pale sunshine.

'Good job I left the skis behind,' thought Arni.

He marched on and on. He seemed the only human being on the white breast of a still, immense ocean of ice and rock, but, bred in the north as he was, Arni was never afraid of space and solitude.

At last, he halted for a short rest. He had been going up and up, and he did not think that he had ever seen that part of his world before. He turned sharply and looked northwards. There, the uplands sloped gently towards the lip of a small lake, its face clear of snow, the ice burning blue and pale green under the sun. Beyond stood a huddle of sharply jagged dark violet rocks, their peaks suggesting a gigantic broken comb. To the east the rocks gave way to an immense forest.

'No use my making for the lake,' thought Arni. 'Oh dear goodness, I think I've walked far enough, and I suppose it is time to turn back, or Mother will fuss – and I have found nothing at all, but where else can I look?'

64

Then he decided he would climb a bit higher and have a last good look all round.

That last lap proved rather steep. At last, however, Arni got to the top and turned to look towards the east. What he saw made him rub his eyes. Was it just a trick played by the sun on the snow? He rubbed his eyes again, he looked hard, and went on looking.

He could no longer doubt what he saw. Down below, to the south-east, all mantled in silver and pink-shining snow, lay Bielostrov. Even at that distance Arni could distinguish some of the familiar landmarks: the fat onion-shaped cupolas of the Russian church, the tall steeple of the Town Hall, the ochre-coloured, sprawling huddle of the station buildings. It looked just as it had always done. From where he stood, Arni could not see the road running between Bielostrov and Raino. He supposed that the hateful barriers and the men with loaded rifles would be there. But little Bielostrov itself seemed just the same – peaceful, and tidy, and a little sleepy – as though it had no concern with wars, revolutions or any such violence. Arni supposed that the kindly red-cheeked lady was still there in her little shop, selling embroidered purses, lengths of pink and blue ribbon, and boxes of coloured beads.

Then, wonder mounting higher and higher, Arni looked to the left of the little town. Beyond the tall steeple of the Town Hall and the station, stretched a great field, and there was the Baroness's Wood. Unaware of his own movement, Arni stepped forward. Here, the ground sloped down to the bank of a narrow river. He moved on until he was able to pick out some more of the landmarks he knew so well – a tumbledown cottage at the very edge of the wood, a great tree split in two by a long forgotten storm, a gap to the right where a broad ride ran through the entire length of the Baroness's Wood.

He had found the way to it. He had never even dared to hope that he would. The only familiar route to Bielostrov lay along the main road, now so tragically forbidden to all peaceful travellers. But he, Arni, had found another way. His heart was like a caged bird. He saw that the west bank of the river was flat. On the other side, it looked a bit steep, but Arni hoped he could manage to climb it. Beyond the east bank a field ran straight into the wood. It would not take him long to cross it.

He stood very still. He realized that the opposite bank lay beyond the frontier, but it seemed completely unguarded. 'Why should those people bother about a wood?' Arni thought, still gazing hungrily. 'It is the town that matters. Here they haven't even put any fencing.'

All his pulses were charged with a sense of an incredible triumph. The snow at his feet, the granite boulders scattered all over the uplands, and the sky overhead heard his shouts of joy. This was the biggest 'secret' he had ever had. Surely, he prayed, the weather would remain kindly to make it possible for him to bring the tree into the house, to watch his father fix the great gilt star, to feel that the Child had come once again.

'If that happens,' Arni whispered, 'why, I would never again be cross with Kesti so long as she doesn't rile me with that stupid doll of hers.'

Flushed with triumph and pride, Arni turned home. He ran almost all the way but even so he was late for the midday meal, and Anna was angry and Kesti in tears by the time he got back. 'If it hadn't been for leaving Kesti alone I'd have gone to the timber-yard to ask Father to look for you,' Anna scolded. 'Did you go down to Raino and stay talking to someone there?'

'No, Mother,' Arni bent his flushed face over the platter. 'Just all over the uplands and there were no snowdrifts.'

'You are never to do it again – not after such a storm, said Anna crossly.

CHAPTER 9

Arni starts his adventure

Biki was the only member of the household that Arni could talk to. He hurried off to the summer house, feeling as if he was almost bursting with his 'secret'.

'I mustn't take you with me, Biki, because you might start barking at a squirrel, and I must keep very, very quiet, but I'll tell you all about it when I get home. Biki, do you know that I saw Bielostrov this morning, the place where Father bought your collar? And it looked just the same – nothing changed, and there was the Baroness's Wood, too . . .'

Arni decided that he must go to the wood on Thursday, the very day when he was invited to eat at Erni's house at Raino. He remembered that he had not told his mother anything about this invitation, and he thought he had better wait till Monday to do so. The invitation was something of a miracle now. Erni's mother would, of course, expect him, Arni, to leave in time to get home by daylight – but even so the journey and the party would mean that he could be away from home for several hours without anyone fussing about him. Next day, he said at supper:

'Oh Mother, I forgot to tell you that Erni's people have asked me to go and eat with them next Thursday. It is his birthday. Erni said there would be plenty of boiled bacon and honey-cakes, too.'

Nils looked pleased. Not so Anna.

'You should have told me before! Why, only three days left, and how can I manage to get you ready for a birthday party? All your hose are darned, and the collar of your best shirt is all frayed, and I'll have to give a good rub to your leather breeches!'

'Mother, it is not a party. It won't matter what I wear.'

'No son of mine goes to a friend's house looking like a beggar,' Anna broke in, 'and you must also think of a present to give to Erni. You can't go empty-handed. I could pack some fresh eggs into a pretty basket for his mother. Have you got a pencil or a penholder to spare for Erni?'

69

'I suppose so,' Arni answered moodily.

How in the world could he go on that important and difficult journey in his best clothes? Suppose he tore the only pair of leather breeches he possessed? And what would he do with a basket of eggs and a parcel for Erni? Why couldn't his mother be reasonable? Trying to keep despair out of his voice Arni said:

'Erni's sure to take me into his father's forge and I'll mess everything up.'

'Not if you are careful,' said Anna, and Arni knew from her voice that there was nothing else he could say.

The next three days were rather a torment for Arni. His mother decided that the collar of his best shirt was past mending, so she cut out a new collar, and made Arni submit to so many fittings that he ended by loathing the shirt. His mother looked through all his hose and said that none of them were tidy enough. She rummaged in her chest, found some green and scarlet wool, and sat deep into the night, her knitting-needles flying. His brown leather breeches were rubbed and rubbed until they shone, and the mere sight of his mother so hard at work made Arni feel uneasy. How in the world would he climb that steep river bank with his best breeches on and wearing such beautiful green hose with scarlet tassels? He pictured himself coming home, the breeches scratched all over and the lovely hose ruined beyond repair. His conscience bit into him, but Arni dared say nothing except to Biki on those rare occasions when he could escape to the summer house. There Biki, his nose against Arni's knee, patiently listened to all the anxieties of those last three days.

To sharpen his discomfort, there was Kesti following him from house to yard and back again, now coaxing him to take her with him, now asking him to promise that he would bring back some honey-cakes for Titi, now simply whimpering, and Arni, remembering his father's threat, had to rein in his temper as best he could.

'Erni asked me to come early, Mother.'

'All right, but remember not to fight or to play rough games. Of course, it all depends on the weather. I'd never let you go if there were a blizzard blowing.'

But the weather remained kindly. Arni could hardly sleep the last night for the excitement, and was up long before dawn. He dressed himself carefully and hid the knife in the deep pocket of his sheepskins. There, too, lay the piece of rope he would need for tying the tree to his little sledge.

Downstairs, on the table lay a pretty basket of eggs and a small parcel for Erni, with a pencil and a painted penholder inside. Arni was no longer worried about the things he was supposed to take to Raino. He had already marked a certain tree with a hollow where he would put both the basket and the parcel. He felt sure that Erni would not mind getting his birthday present a few days late. At the very last moment his parents wanted to know why Arni was taking the little sledge.

'Why, just in case I see some wood for the fire on the way back,' he answered. 'And I am not taking Biki – there's that mastiff at the forge. Biki and he might start a fight.'

'Mind the basket,' said Anna. 'Come back by daylight, give our respects to everybody, and be sure to thank Erni's mother after the meal.

He was off. While still within sight of the house, he turned to the left once he got near the wood. A few minutes later he knew he was safe. He doubled on his tracks and pushed on. The going proved far easier than it had done the first time. Arni marched on, starry-eyed, pulling the little sledge behind him. From time to time he fingered the knife in his pocket, making certain that it was still there.

It was one of those all too rare wintry days in the North when the very frost in the air breathed with a caress. The sun glanced off tree and shrub and boulder, and veined them all with fugitive gold. The snow felt firm and yet smooth under his feet. A south-west breeze met him on the uplands. The sky was a great cup of such a delicate blue that he knew he could never have matched it in his paint-box. The blue deepened slightly towards the west, but Arni, bred in that country, could tell that no threat of any blizzard need be feared on such a day.

As he plodded on, he thought of many things, and suddenly he remembered a story told by the teacher almost a year ago. It was a very old legend, she told them, and she had such a way with her that, as soon as she had begun, she drew them all into the heart of the story. It was about the three kings travelling to Bethlehem to greet the Child, and they were taking gifts to Him, gold, frankincense and myrrh. In the story, the three presents, each cradled in a coffer of precious wood, began talking one to another. Frankincense considered itself to be the most important gift among the three since it was offered in worship to God, but gold pointed out that it alone was a fit present for a king. Myrrh tried to say something too, but the other two at once silenced it. 'You – you are just something people bring to a funeral. We can't understand why you should be offered as a gift to a king. How dare you speak to us?' And myrrh held its peace.

The three kings reached Bethlehem, and found the Child and His mother. They opened their precious coffers, and frankincense expected to be the first to be accepted by the Child, and so did gold. But the Child, having looked at the three coffers, at once stretched out His hand for the humble myrrh.

Now Arni was at the very top of the uplands, and he threw a glance eastwards. Bielostrov lay in the pale sunshine, looking very peaceful. Arni came nearer the bank of the river, and he remembered the old carol they would surely sing the very next evening. There, with the narrow river just below him, Arni knew he dared not sing it aloud, much though he wanted to, but the lines which he knew by heart went flowing through his memory:

Small will you find Him,
Humble and helpless,
Small in His Mother's arms,
Lord of all things.

Seas live in praise of Him,
Forests and mountains,
Sun and moon worship Him,
Stars sing His name;

Worlds we know nothing of
Worship the Word,

Who from a Maiden pure
Took our poor flesh.

In the Lord's smallness, then,
Let our pride die,
Like a spring runnel that
Dies in the sea.

In your great smallness, Lord,
Use our poor praise
Till the dark, tired earth
Shines with your light,

And in that shining, Lord,
The night will die,
Like a spring runnel that
Dies in the sea.

Arni went through all the familiar verses, and the old carol lent him the courage he needed at that moment. He crossed the river easily, but the other bank proved far more difficult than he had thought. It rose steep and jagged, not a shrub anywhere, nothing but sharp-edged pieces of granite boulders swept clear of snow and coated with treacherous ice. Arni was sure-footed enough, but that climb tested his skill to the utmost. He nearly slipped once or twice, and the little sledge he was pulling hampered him badly, but he knew he would never be able to bring the tree down in his arms. He would need one hand free for the descent.

'It's sure to be easier on the way down,' he comforted himself as he hoisted the sledge to the very top.

Now nothing but a field lay between Arni and the Baroness's Wood. He looked about. Not a sign of anyone and not a sound reached him. He ran towards the wood, his heart singing within him. Soon he came upon a shapely little fir about four or five feet high, and he knelt in the snow, his gauntleted hands brushing against the delicate fronds. Then he stood up and fumbled in his pocket for the knife.

It was not there.

For a moment Arni stood rooted to the ground, despair engulfing him from head to foot. He had fingered the knife all the way along, that he knew. He just could not have dropped it anywhere – but it had gone. He must now retrace his steps and he must hurry, too, to get back before dusk fell. Dumbly Arni prayed that he might find the knife somewhere across the field on the way back to the river. Yes, surely, he must have dropped it there. His mind was so full of the old carol that he might not have noticed anything falling out of the pocket.

That seemed but a slender hope, but Arni clutched it hard as he turned back. He must hurry, and yet he could not hurry because his eyes scanned every inch of the ground. Nowhere could he see the sheath of faded crimson. The field behind him, he came to the top of the bank and looked over. The crimson sheath was there – lying at the very bottom of the bank.

Arni clenched his teeth as he began the descent. Clutching hard at a stone, he knew he had torn the thumb of his left gauntlet, but he was past caring about the state of his clothes. He inched his way down, his little face grim, his mouth a taut thin line. He picked up the knife and decided to carry it between his teeth for greater safety.

He could not hurry back to the wood. His knees were shaking and his arms ached as though he had been carrying a great burden for a long time. Arni waited a few moments before ascending the bank for the second time.

That proved even worse, and Arni never knew how he managed it. Sometimes he went on his hands and knees. Sometimes he sprawled on his tummy to reach for the next boulder across his way. When, all but exhausted, he hoisted himself to the top, he felt something hot and sticky trickling down his left leg. He had grazed his shin against some sharp stone. The beautiful green stocking had a gaping rent from the knee down to the top of the snowboot. Arni looked at the gash almost indifferently, mopped up the blood with his handkerchief, and crossed the field for the third time. Another couple of minutes, and he was kneeling by the little tree he had chosen. Carefully, remembering the way his father did it, Arni began cutting at the slim trunk some four or five inches above the ground. His breath came and went jerkily, and his fingers were numb by the time he had finished and the little tree lay on the ground beside him.

'Now back to the sledge,' Arni muttered to himself and was just about to get up when a heavy hand clutched his left shoulder and a gruff voice asked in Russian:

'Now then, you young limb of Satan, what tricks are you up to? Stealing our timber, eh?'

CHAPTER 10

Arni is made prisoner

Arni's blood froze. He never knew how he managed to turn round.

A tall bearded man in a greatcoat, a rifle slung over his shoulder, towered over him. The fur helmet the man wore came so low over his forehead that Arni could not see his eyes very clearly but he felt they were anything but friendly. The huge gauntleted hand still clutched Arni's shoulder in a grip that hurt. He moistened his lips nervously but he could not speak.

77

'Are you dumb then?' the man shook him.

Arni struggled to recover his voice. It came in a husky, broken whisper:

'Please, I am no thief . . . Oh please . . .'

'No thief? You would say that! And not a Russian boy either, are you?'

Arni had not enough energy to shake his head.

'No thief?' repeated the man. 'You come and tell the pretty story to my friend, and we'll sort it out together. No thief, and a tree cut down! Don't you know what stealing means?' Still holding tight to Arni, the man stooped and picked up the little tree so roughly that some of the delicate branches snapped in two. Arni's heart ached when he saw it.

'Come along,' the man thundered at him.

They moved into the wood, going down the lovely wide ride that Arni remembered well from his earlier visits. He stumbled as he went. His feet dragged. His fear held him in hoops of iron. The man, now silent, walked faster and faster, and soon Arni had to run beside him. Half-way down the ride the man swung to the right, and Arni saw a small timbered hut standing in a clearing. He had never seen the hut before, and he thought that the men who had put up the barriers must have built it.

The giant pushed at the door with his booted foot and shouted:

'Here, Aleshka, a fish in our net at last! I've caught a thief – red-handed, too.'

The hut was small and almost unbearably hot. In it were a trestle and a table, and a stool by the large iron stove, the funnel

78

of which was thrust through the wall. Another giant, his curly dark head bare, got to his feet.

'That?' he gave a contemptuous glance at Arni. 'And what's he been stealing, Petka?'

'Here it is,' Petka tossed the little fir on the floor. As it fell, a number of the slender branches snapped, and Arni could not bear to look at it any longer.

'Well, now!' said Aleshka, contempt deepening in his dark brown eyes. 'Fancy anyone being stupid enough to run their head into a noose for a silly little fir! Where do you come from?' he asked Arni. 'And mind you tell us the truth, do you hear?'

'From Raino,' Arni whispered, and Petka cut in:

'He is a Finnish brat, Aleshka. He can't speak our language properly.'

'What does your father do?'

'He – he works at a timber-yard.'

'Ah, and you help him, don't you? And he sent you along to steal the timber, eh? Not enough trees in that precious proud country of yours and you have to sneak across the frontier and help yourselves to what is ours, is that it?'

'No, no! My father – didn't know – anything . . .'

'Didn't I tell you to speak the truth?' Aleshka shouted, and Arni could no longer keep his tears back. They came gushing. But the men stared at him coldly.

'Stop snivelling,' Petka said roughly. 'How many trees were you after?'

'One – just one – '

Petka swore under his breath and Aleshka stamped his foot.

'You want us to believe that you tramped all the way here to get one miserable little fir?'

Arni gulped.

'You – you said I was to speak the truth.'

'Listen, stupid, do you know who we are? We are frontier guards, and we go about armed, and it is our job to shoot anyone sneaking across the way you've done, see? And how did you know the way?'

Arni gulped again.

'I've – I've been here before,' he stammered. 'It's the Baroness's Wood . . . She allows it . . . '

'Hang the Baroness – whoever she is! There are no baronesses or countesses now. The wood belongs to the State, see?'

Arni did not quite see. He stood silent.

'Petka,' Aleshka turned to his comrade, 'we'll sort it out carefully, but I think the lad's hungry.'

'So am I,' Petka retorted, crossing the room to a cupboard in a corner and helping himself to some food.

'Let the boy have a bit,' said Aleshka.

Petka shrugged.

'Please yourself – but I'd rather he had none of my grub.'

'There's enough of mine,' Aleshka flung over his shoulder, and brought out some bread, a plate of pickled mushrooms and a small slice of cold bacon. He put the food on the table and said gruffly:

'Come and eat, you stupid.'

Arni tottered towards the table. In spite of the heat in the hut, his hands were so cold that he could hardly hold the bacon. He was sunk in misery and fear. He hated the men, but hunger would not be denied and he relished the food. The last scrap eaten, he said shyly:

'Thank you.'

'Got some manners, haven't you?' Aleshka lit a cigarette and leant against the wall. 'Now what are we going to do with you?'

Arni swallowed a difficult breath.

'Please, could I – go home?'

Aleshka frowned and Petka burst into loud, unkind laughter.

'That's a good one! Oh yes, my little gentleman, we'll put you into a big sledge, cover you up with a fur rug and send you home with our compliments, yes, and have a hundred firs cut for you into the bargain.'

'Be quiet,' said Aleshka, 'can't you see the lad's scared enough as it is?'

'And he'll be scared a bit more before we have done with him,' Petka retorted, his eyes blazing with anger. 'Send him home indeed! No, my lad, we've short shrift for people who come sneaking across the border.'

Here Arni remembered all his father had said. His eyes wide with terror, he almost tumbled off the trestle and clutched at the table.

'Please, please,' he gasped. 'You can't . . . You won't . . . It was all for the Child.'

'What child?' Aleshka, the cigarette out of his mouth, stared at Arni, and Petka said cuttingly:

'Whose child?'

Arni hung his head. It was all so simple, he had lived with it all his life, but he found it hard to explain, and Petka jeered at him:

'Gone dumb again, have you?'

'No, it's the Child, and – and – Christmas – and – the Star – ' stumblingly, slowly, often pausing for a word in the language he did not really know well, Arni began the old, old story about the inn refusing shelter to tired travellers. He spoke of the oxen, asses and camels crowding round about the stall where the young Mother bent over her Child, of the shepherds running in, and the three kings bringing their gifts. As Arni went on, he almost forgot his terror. He felt as though the Child had accepted that all but broken little tree, wet with the melted snow clinging to its fronds, with neither star nor candle to do it honour.

Aleshka kept still, the ash of his cigarette growing longer and longer, but Petka kept crossing and uncrossing his legs, and at last he broke in:

'Touching, isn't it? And then everything in the garden is lovely – with roses tumbling down from heaven, or is it violets?'

Arni knit his forehead.

'It – isn't a bit like that . . . I try not to tease Kesti – she's my sister – so much, or make Mother wait for the kindling, and – and all that sort of thing. For twelve evenings we keep lighting the twelve candles, and we sing a little.' His voice broke off as he remembered it all.

'I see,' Petka smirked, 'and you believe all that old rubbish, do you?'

'Be quiet,' Aleshka muttered, and Arni's eyes opened wide with wonder.

'But it is all true. There – there would be just nothing if the

Child were not there,' he stuttered, all words running away from him. He had told them everything he could, and he was almost past caring what happened to him. He tried to get up and he could not. His head fell on his chest. The heat in the hut became a warm blanket all over him. He slipped off the trestle down to the floor and fell into a sleep.

CHAPTER II

'Where is Arni?'

At the very time when Arni was scrambling up the river bank on the way to the Baroness's Wood, Nils ran across the little yard, shouting:

'Anna, Anna, such wonderful news! I had to run back and tell you all about it at once.'

Anna pulled a pot away from the fire and rushed to the door where Nils, his eyes shining, stood thumping the caked snow off his boots.

'You have got that job near Helsinki?' she cried.

'Much better than that,' he flung his arms round her neck. 'No, dear wife, we shan't now have to give up our home. Mr Pitoen has found a way out of his difficulties! He's got four new contracts and a promise of several more – all to the west of Raino. This means a six-day week for me again, and he's taking all his old hands back again. Now you'll have a new shawl and boots, and that young rascal of ours had better be measured for new sheep-skins. By the way, where is he?'

'Surely, you haven't forgotten? He's gone to Erni's birthday dinner. Oh Nils, my dear, I prayed so hard that we might weather this troubled time, and now I just can't believe it,' Anna cried and laughed at the same time, and Nils hugged her.

'You'll know it is true when I start spending the money. Now give me a kiss, and something to eat too, and then I must be off.'

Anna ran to fetch the loaf and some cheese. From a corner came Kesti's voice:

'Has something nice happened, Father? Titi is pleased. She wants a new petticoat.'

'I'll give her three petticoats,' laughed Nils, wolfing his bread and cheese, and then he was off again.

'And what is the nice thing?' asked Kesti.

'Your father has got plenty of work again, little one. There'll be nuts and caramels for Christmas now, and I'll bake some ginger-cakes, and we'll fix the star and the candlesticks all round the room, and pretend the tree is there.'

'The tree will be there,' said Kesti. 'Arni promised me.'

Anna was startled. 'What are you talking about, little one?'

But Kesti remembered that she had promised not to tell. She dug her spoon into her stew and muttered:

'I don't know and Titi does not know.'

When she had cleared the table, Anna sat down to her knitting, and the needles flew in her hands. Not to see that worried look in her husband's eyes seemed the finest Christmas present she could have had.

Daylight ebbed away. Anna walked to the door and peered into the cold, dark green dusk. There seemed no sign of Arni. She closed the door, her brow furrowed in wonder rather than anxiety. But the time passed, and she was about to light the candle when Nils came in. Anna tried to keep anxiety out of her voice when she said:

'Surely, Erni's parents would have sent our boy home before dark.'

'Don't you worry, Anna. You know what boys are like. He and Erni probably started a new game just before dusk, and don't forget that our lad knows every inch of the way.'

'I do wish Arni had taken Biki with him,' Anna sighed, as she set the candlestick on a little bracket near the stove, and just at that moment Biki, who had been asleep in his corner, stirred, sat up on his haunches, and gave a long howl. Anna's face went white.

'Nils,' she whispered, 'you haven't heard – I mean – there haven't been any rumours of wolves in the neighbourhood?'

Nils shook his head.

'Not one heard of this side of Tavashust,' he said hurriedly, 'but, if you like, I could ski down to Raino. I'll probably run into the boy on the way and give him a good telling off,' and he was starting to move to the door when Biki howled again and yet again. Anna clutched at the back of the rocking-chair, her lips ashen.

'Nils, something has happened to Arni on the way back from Raino, and Biki knows it. He is so clever – he'd never howl for nothing.'

'Now don't you talk such nonsense. It's probably a fox prowling about in the wood. The hens are all shut up, though,' and Nils went.

Anna kept very still. From the top of the little stairway came Kesti's voice asking for Arni.

'Father has gone to meet him, little one. Go back to bed.'

'It is so cold for Titi upstairs.'

'Wrap her up and she'll be warm.'

'And why is Biki howling?'

'There's probably a fox running about in the wood. Father is going to see to it when he gets back.'

'May Titi come downstairs? She'll keep very quiet, Mother.'

'All right,' Anna said wearily.

Kesti, with Titi wrapped in a bright blue scarf, settled down by the stove and kept very quiet indeed. Biki stopped howling. Tense and cold, Anna waited. She dared not glance at the white wooden face of the little clock. The room was still except for the occasional crackle of a log. Anna had to wait some time. When Nils came back, she had hardly the strength to get up when she saw that he was alone, but he beckoned to her. Forgetting all about shawls and coats Anna ran through the door into the cold, dark porch.

'I don't want Kesti to be scared,' Nils whispered hurriedly. 'Anna, Arni's never been to Raino at all. I ran into Erni's father just before I got there, and I made a joke of it all. I said he'd been kept very busy and I told him I was so sorry we couldn't send a message. We mustn't make a fool of the boy by fussing all over the place. But he could never have lost his way to Raino in the morning. He must have gone somewhere else.'

87

Anna's shoulders shook as a thought occurred to her.

'Kesti told me that he'd promised her a tree, Nils, and it's Christmas Eve tomorrow.'

'What?' Nils gasped. 'He'd never be such a fool as to go to the Baroness's Wood!'

'How can I tell? How can you tell?' Anna clung to Nils, 'And if they caught him – '

'Steady, steady,' he flung his arm about her shoulders. 'Let's go in and ask Kesti.'

Kesti looked deeply ashamed of herself. She had promised not to tell, she whimpered, but Arni said they would have their tree, and she burst into tears.

Nils stood by the table, his head bent.

'He must have gone there, wife,' he said at last. 'There is nothing else for it – I must make for Bielostrov and ask them to let me in to look for him. Even the Russians couldn't imagine that such a little lad got in to spy on them.'

'But they'd never let you out again,' Anna cried, when suddenly Biki sprang up, gave a loud bark, and bounced towards the door. So eager was he to get out that Nils opened the door for him, and Biki rushed past him into the dark. Through the open door the tinkle of a sledge bell reached them.

CHAPTER 12

The hour of the little tree

Arni woke up with a start, his legs and arms so numb that they seemed made of wood. He raised his head, bumped it against a leg of the table, and for a moment he could not tell where he was. Then he saw Aleshka by the stove, a cigarette between his lips, his long legs stretched out, and the horror of it all came back to Arni. Wildly, he stared at the small oil lamp swinging from the ceiling. It was lit. How long had he slept? The day was gone. What would be happening at home?

He continued to stare about. Petka was not there, and the poor damaged tree had gone, too. Panting and gasping, Arni struggled to his feet.

'Please,' he stammered, 'oh please, will you let me go home?'

'All by yourself in the dark?' Aleshka spoke gruffly, his dark eyes staring at the logs in the stove. 'What do you take me for, lad? Well, you've slept long enough. I was just about to wake you up. Listen, you scamp, I am taking you home.'

89

Arni's legs were trembling so that he had to sit down on the trestle.

'But you can't – it's right across the frontier – and. . .'

'Don't you argue,' Aleshka broke in, lighting another cigarette. 'I know every inch of the way, and your men aren't like ours – they don't have their eyes skinned for any spot of trouble. And if anything happened,' he shrugged, 'well, it would be sort of tit for tat, eh? But there's plenty of time to worry about trouble when it's there and not before.' Aleshka took a long puff at his cigarette and added:

'Want any more food, do you?'

Arni shook his head. He still could not believe it.

'When you were asleep,' Aleshka went on conversationally, 'I went back into the wood and I cut you a better fir. I found your little sledge, too. I've just harnessed the pony to my big sledge, and it won't take us long to get there, but mind you never try such a trick again. I'd no end of a job with Petka. He wanted things done differently.'

'Please,' Arni faltered, 'where is he?'

'I've sent him packing,' Aleshka answered loftily. 'I am senior to him – not that he always remembers it – and in the end I just told him to stop arguing, but it took some time, I can tell you. Petka's a very hard man. I suppose you've got to be hard for this job,' and Aleshka shook his head.

Arni still wondered if he were awake or asleep.

'But why – why?' he faltered.

Aleshka broke in: 'Why does snow fall in winter? Take what comes along, lad, and don't waste your breath on too many questions. You've talked quite enough as it is. Now wrap yourself up properly. It's a cruel, cold evening.'

In a few moments, still moving as though he were in a dream, Arni came out of the hut. It was good and more than good to breathe the clean, cold air again after the unbearable stuffiness of the little place. The sky was blazing with stars, and it seemed as though all of them had gathered together to watch Arni regain his freedom. Aleshka swung a lantern shoulder-high, and Arni saw a shaggy pony and a big sledge, more than half-filled with hay, and there was his own little sledge, the shapely little tree carefully laid across it. Arni pinched himself hard. Could it be real, or was it all a lovely dream, and would he wake to hear Petka's terrible voice threatening to shoot him?

It was real. He got into the sledge, and wisps of hay tickled his bare flesh where the stocking had been torn. Arni closed his eyes for a moment for the sheer relief of it all. The pony moved off, and at once a thin plaintive jingle broke upon the stillness, and Aleshka grumbled:

'I forgot to muffle the clapper! Never mind, though! All your people have bells on their sledges, don't they?'

When they had left the wood behind, Aleshka swung sharply to the right, and Arni knew they were not going through Bielostrov, but he asked no questions. The sledge made a wide detour before they crossed the little river at a spot much farther south than that used by Arni earlier in the day. Within a few minutes they were running along the main road to Raino.

'As easy as buttering a bun,' said Aleshka. 'Now we are in your own country, lad. I bet you feel like singing, eh?'

'Yes,' Arni admitted shyly.

'Then sing something. I like a good tune.'

Arni thought for a moment. Then he began the old carol. He reached the end of the second verse and stopped. He could never have found proper words to describe it, but he sensed with every pulse of his body and every thought in his mind that he had indeed found the Child in the kindness of a man, an enemy, who was taking him home at some risk to himself. Then Arni heard Aleshka say:

'A grand little tune indeed, but what was it all about? I don't know your language, lad.'

'About the little Lord being born and all the stars singing to Him.'

'Well,' said Aleshka in an oddly tautened voice, 'I don't know about their singing, but they are certainly blazing brightly tonight.'

Presently Arni saw a glimmering light to the left across the brook, and Aleshka reined in.

'That your place, lad? Quite sure you will find your way from here? No, wait a moment, let me turn her round. I'll have to get off double-quick,' he laughed. 'Here, let me get your sledge out. Be careful with the little fir, now. I couldn't cut you another, eh?'

Arni jumped down. He could not see Aleshka's face. He stretched up and fumbled for the big gauntleted hand and stammered, the words coming from his very heart:

'Thank you,' and once again, 'thank you.'

'Oh, that's nothing. Now mind, never do it again and mind,

too, that you stick to the story you told us. I reckon it did me a power of good to hear it.'

The sledge moved off into the dark, and at once the jingle of the bell was drowned in furious barking.

'Biki, Biki,' shouted Arni, and Aleshka drove off at a furious pace.

*

Arni rushed forward, Biki nearly sweeping him off his feet. At last, panting and crying, he left the little sledge in the yard, and burst through the doorway.

'I am so sorry, so sorry, I couldn't help it, I promised, I had to do it,' he gulped and stammered, and Anna had him in her arms and hugged him so tight that he could hardly breathe for a moment. Presently, the whole story tumbled out, and the frown on Nils's face gave way to something like a look of pride, but Anna could not take much of it in. She kept crying and catching hold of Arni's hands and stroking his cheek and crying again.

'But you haven't got your tree,' said Nils, and Arni cried:

'Oh yes I have, Father.'

He was out like lightning. He made for the summer house, found the stand, and ran back to the yard to untie the little fir. When he brought it into the house, Anna stood up. Suddenly down the stairs came Kesti in her funny pink nightgown. She looked at the shapely little tree and said:

'I knew you would keep your promise, Arni. You always do. And now the Child will come.'

The little clock struck midnight. Anna mounted the stairs and returned with the oblong wooden box in her arms. Nils fixed the tree to the stand, and Arni helped him with the star and the twelve little candlesticks. Anna closed the stove doors and snuffed out the big candle on the bracket. Then she raised her hand and they began the old carol. They would have sung it to the end but Biki's madly joyous barking drowned their voices at the second verse.

The Author

E. M. ALMEDINGEN was born in St. Petersburg, Russia, where she attended the Xenia Nobility School and the University of Petrograd. She lectured on English Medieval History and Literature at the university from 1920 to 1922. A year later Miss Almedingen went to England, where she has lived ever since except for periods of travel throughout Europe and parts of Asia.

Since leaving Russia Miss Almedingen has devoted herself to writing and lecturing. In 1951, she was lecturer in Russian Literature at Oxford, and she is a fellow of the Royal Society of Literature. To date she has written more than twenty-five books of poetry, fiction, and nonfiction, including her autobiography *Tomorrow Will Come,* a recent biography *The Romanovs,* and several books for children, among them *The Treasure of Siegfried* and *Knights of the Golden Table* and *The Story of Gudrun.*

Now a British citizen, Miss Almedingen lives in Somerset.